# MOUSE ISLAND

# MOUSE ISLAND

EVE BUNTING

PICTURES BY DOMINIC CATALANO

BOYDS MILLS PRESS
HONESDALE, PENNSYLVANIA

*For Midge, who loves my mouse*
*and all living things*
　　　　　—E.B.

*For my boys, Peter and Cristian,*
*who fill up my life with joy!*
　　　　　—D.C.

Text copyright © 2008 by Eve Bunting
Illustrations copyright © 2008 by Dominic Catalano
All rights reserved

Boyds Mills Press, Inc.
815 Church Street
Honesdale, Pennsylvania 18431
Printed in China

Library of Congress Cataloging-in-Publication Data

Bunting, Eve.
  Mouse island / Eve Bunting ; illustrated by
Dominic Catalano.—1st ed.
      p. cm.
  Summary: Mouse enjoys living on his island but
feels that something is missing from his life until
the day he performs a daring rescue and acquires an
unlikely friend.
  ISBN 978-1-59078-447-1 (hardcover : alk. paper)
[1. Mice—Fiction. 2. Islands—Fiction. 3. Contentment—
Fiction. 4. Rescues—Fiction. 5. Cats—
Fiction.]  I. Catalano, Dominic, ill. II. Title.

  PZ7.B91527Mq 2008
  [E]—dc22
                                    2007017558

First edition
The text of this book is set in
  16-point Century Schoolbook.
The illustrations are done in pastels.

10 9 8 7 6 5 4 3 2 1

Mouse lived alone on an island.

Once a keeper and his wife had lived in the big lighthouse, but they were no longer needed. Now the great light turned on and off by itself. In the night, its beam still flashed white across the ocean:

ATTENTION ALL SHIPS! DANGER!

Sometimes storms snarled and spat at his island.
But Mouse was safe.

On days when the ocean licked calm against his beach,
Mouse tiptoed among the tide pools, nibbling the soft-bellied
sea things that clung to the rocks, or slept, warm in the sun.

He saw whales passing, their white breaths smoking against the sky.

Sea lions, fat and whiskered, honked at him and at one another.

Every day Mouse wondered why he wasn't the most contented mouse on earth. Why did he always feel that there was something missing in his life?

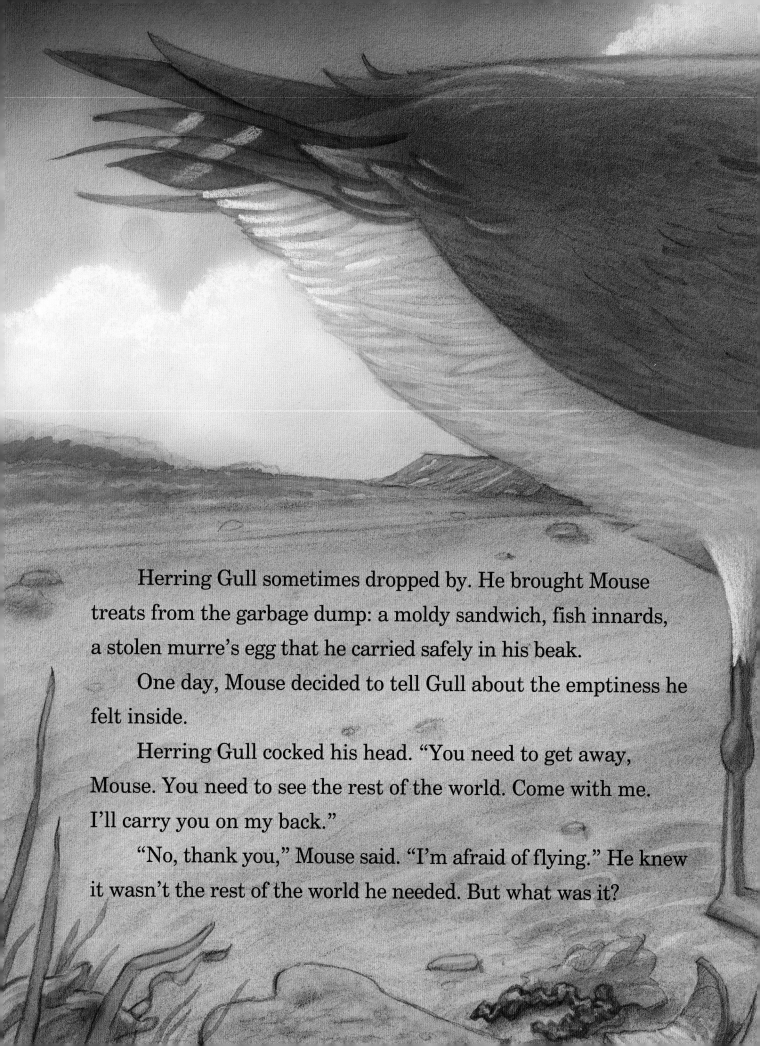

Herring Gull sometimes dropped by. He brought Mouse treats from the garbage dump: a moldy sandwich, fish innards, a stolen murre's egg that he carried safely in his beak.

One day, Mouse decided to tell Gull about the emptiness he felt inside.

Herring Gull cocked his head. "You need to get away, Mouse. You need to see the rest of the world. Come with me. I'll carry you on my back."

"No, thank you," Mouse said. "I'm afraid of flying." He knew it wasn't the rest of the world he needed. But what was it?

One sunny afternoon, he sat gnawing a strip of salty orange peel that had washed ashore. He liked to watch the fishing boats way out on the horizon. Suddenly, he realized one was sinking!

Mouse threw down his orange peel. What could he do?

"Help!" he yelled in his loudest mouse voice. "Somebody help!"

And then he saw a lifeboat rushing across the water on wings of foam. He watched as three men were lifted to safety. But still, there was one head in the water. It was too small for the head of a person.

"Hold on!" Mouse shouted as he plunged in. "I'm coming!"

Sea filled his nose and mouth. His fur was waterlogged. Mouse had taught himself to swim in the small tide pools, but he'd never been in the ocean before. It was scary. Waves lifted him and smashed him back down. With his tail as a rudder, he steered toward the bobbing black head and paddled water, gulping, gasping, staring. What kind of sea creature was this? Whatever it was, it was in trouble.

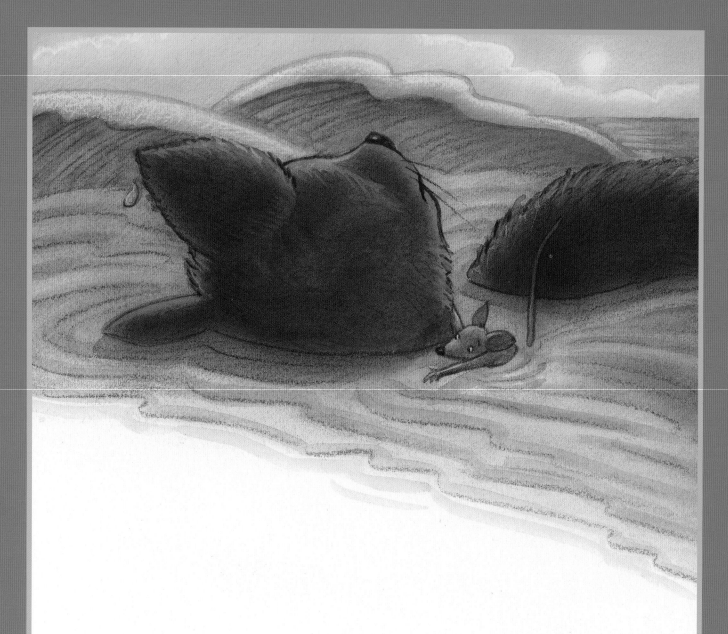

Mouse put his paw under the furry chin and stroked for shore. Oh, the creature was heavy! So heavy!

At last his mouse feet touched land and he dragged the half-drowned creature behind him, pulling and tugging, stopping every few steps to rest. He laid it on the sand.

"Oh my!" he whispered, walking around it. "What have I got here?"

Suddenly, big green eyes opened. Water spurted from a wide cave of a mouth. Mouse saw sharp, pointy teeth.

He stepped back.

"*Meow!*" the creature said.

"Are you . . . are you all right?" Mouse quivered.

The creature's eyes narrowed. "Do you know who I am?"

Mouse shook his head.

"I am Cat. Cat eats mouse."

"Oh-oh!" Mouse got ready to run. "Are you hungry? I could offer you a nice ruffled jellyfish. I'll just get it from . . ."

A gigantic paw came down on his back, pinning him to the sand.

"Don't leave," Cat said. "We need to talk. Do you live here on the island?"

Mouse nodded.

"Alone?"

"Yes."

Cat lifted his paw so Mouse was free. "Do you like it here?"

"Yes." He didn't tell Cat of the emptiness inside him. "I hope you don't have an emptiness inside *you*, Cat," he whispered.

"I have," Cat said. "But don't worry. I would never eat *you*. You saved me. You offered me food. You invited me to your island. I am an honorable cat and I have an obligation."

"I can teach you to fish," Mouse said. "Does Cat eat fish?"

"Cat loves fish. Just not jellyfish."

They walked, one behind
the other.

"By the way," Cat asked,
"do you play beach volleyball?"

Mouse shook his head.

"Never mind," Cat said.
"I can teach you."

Mouse smiled.

His island sparkled and shone. And now he had a friend to share it. He thought how strange it was that sometimes you didn't know what you wanted till you found it. And then you knew it was what you wanted all the time.